HAPPY HATCHLINGS

The tale of six happy hatchling turtles

Written and illustrated by Sue Trew

Thank you to my friend and neighbour Hazel Oxenford, PhD
for sharing her love and knowledge of our remarkable marine world
and for working with me to combine education with adventure to make learning fun.

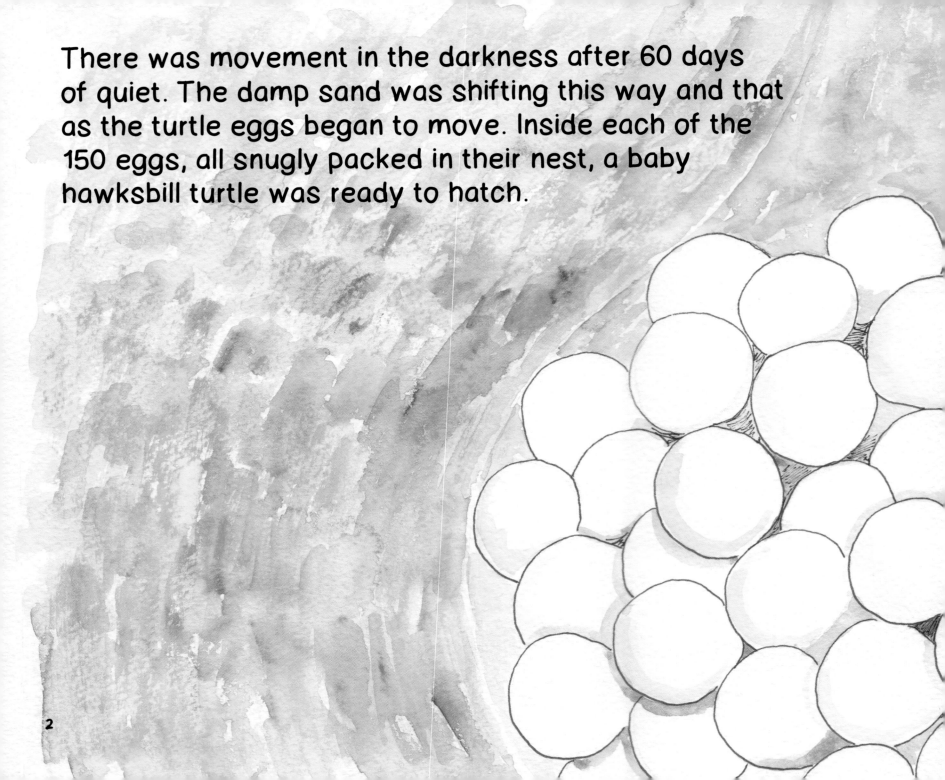

There was movement in the darkness after 60 days of quiet. The damp sand was shifting this way and that as the turtle eggs began to move. Inside each of the 150 eggs, all snugly packed in their nest, a baby hawksbill turtle was ready to hatch.

Using his special egg tooth, the first baby turtle tore a hole in the leathery eggshell, pushing it open with his powerful front flippers.

3

Spurred on by this activity, a second followed and then another until - after three days and nights - the nest was a mass of wriggling sandy hatchlings, making their way up towards the surface, leaving their crumpled egg shells behind.

4

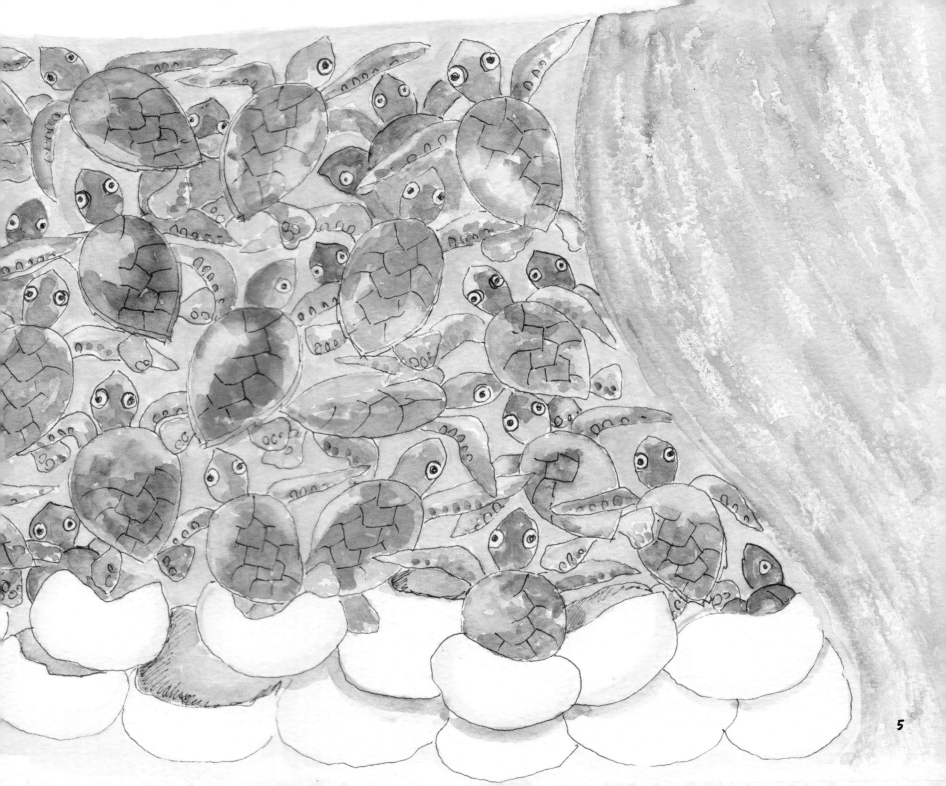

Among them were six very happy hatchlings - Zoom, Buzz, Star, Nibbles, Moonlight and Bump - and they were all waiting ... waiting just below the hot beach sand until they felt it begin to cool, as the sun set.

6

Then - and only then - would they emerge and rush down the beach to the water's edge for the very first time.

7

Zoom surfaced first, tumbling out onto the deserted beach. He took a deep breath of cool sea air and blinked away the sand covering his eyes. He could hear the waves lapping gently on the shore nearby and see the faint glow out to sea where the sun had just gone down ... and he knew what he had to do. He must dash to the sea as fast as his little flippers would carry him - and he was hoping to be the first to get wet!

Buzz was next. Pulling himself upwards, his front flippers moving quickly left, right, left, right until - in a moment - he was out and following Zoom over the firm beach sand. Could he catch him? He was going to try!

More and more emerged. Star found herself pushed up on a tide of wriggling hatchlings and shifting sand as they erupted onto the beach. She overbalanced and fell backwards. Pausing briefly to catch her breath, she began rocking this way and that - waving her strong little flippers - until she tipped herself back onto her tummy.

Moonlight tumbled out near her - thump! - closely
followed by Nibbles. That was fun! Then they were off,
racing down the beach among a mass of other hatchlings,
fanning out as they went. They were excited to be on
their way to the sea.

13

The nest was quiet and almost invisible now the
hatchlings had gone. Suddenly the sand shifted
very slightly and another little head popped up!
It was Bump.

14

Tired and alone, he hauled himself out of the sandy nest. Where was everyone? Looking around he spotted a bright light and headed towards it. The light was coming from a beach house and - oh, no! - it was leading Bump the wrong way. Luckily, some children found him and - very carefully - carried him to a darker part of the beach, setting him down facing the sea.

Hooray! Down the beach he hurried,
following the mass of tiny turtle tracks.
"Wait for me!" he called, keen to join
the other hatchlings in the sea.

Far ahead, Zoom didn't hear him.
He'd reached the water's edge first
and - despite being tumbled a few
times by the breaking waves - he
was now paddling hard out to sea.

Suddenly, Zoom felt afraid. A large and curious eye paused next to him and glinted, then - swoosh! - it was gone in a flash of orange, replaced by another and yet another. Zoom gasped.

18

A shoal of inquisitive ballyhoo surrounded him, their orange tipped swords like a mass of tiny torches showing him the way. "How beautiful they are", thought Zoom, forgetting to be frightened.

Buzz was playing in the surf. He soared over the crest of a wave, catching it perfectly just before it broke. A shoal of young palometa, swimming in the shallows, darted beneath him. "Yippee!" he shouted.

Buzz swam out over the next wave.
He stopped abruptly and stared. Below
him was a magnificent flying gurnard with
its large wing-like fins extended. Was he going
to fly? As Buzz watched, the fish appeared to
crawl forwards, churning up the sand with
its little finger-like fins, looking for food.
It wasn't flying at all!

"Humph!" thought Buzz scornfully, "A fish with beautiful wings that would rather crawl than fly!" and went off to catch another wave.

Star was excited to be in the water. She had come racing down the beach with Nibbles and Moonlight and they'd arrived at the sea together. Now she was out in front showing off her swimming strokes and her pretty style.

Soon the breaking waves were behind her
and Star found herself in calmer water.
It was getting dark and a mass of tiny,
bright stars began to fill the sky.
"How they twinkle," thought Star.
She tucked in her front flippers and
paddled on using her back ones.

She gazed down in amazement at the seagrass beds below her. They too were scattered with stars - but these were big and orange with dotted patterns made of creamy blunt spines. They were West Indian sea stars - and how brilliant they were!

Baby Moonlight saw the stars in the sky too, but something else caught her eye; a large orange ball seemed to be rising out of the sea. It was the full moon - the same moon she was named after. Moonlight watched in wonder as the light from the moon touched the waves, spreading across the water to where she was floating.

A long journey lay ahead of her and the other hatchlings. As she gazed at the rising moon and the sky full of stars, she made a promise to herself to return to this beach one day to lay her very own eggs.

Like the other hatchlings, Nibbles wasn't hungry yet.
She still felt full from absorbing the yolk in her egg.
This would sustain her for the first few days of her life.
It was more urgent that she find a safe place in which
to hide. She spotted a patch of floating sargassum
seaweed and swam towards it.

Hiding in the coppery brown leaves, her front flippers by her side, she noticed a clump of tiny flyingfish eggs. They were just beginning to hatch! Nibbles watched as - one by one - the tiny fish emerged and took shelter in the seaweed. They were too small as yet to venture far.

But where was Bump?
Lots of families had enjoyed
the beach that day and Bump now found
himself stuck in one of the footprints left
behind. How tired he felt. He could hear the sea,
but how was he going to reach it?

Help came in an unlikely form. A little ghost crab emerged from her burrow inside the same footprint. She made a track as she scurried sideways on her eight quickly moving legs. Bump followed the track and soon felt the cool seawater wash over him. He had made it!

He saw Buzz on the next wave and shouted out to him. They swam together, catching up with Star, Nibbles and Moonlight. Then Zoom appeared. He hadn't gone very far ahead after all.

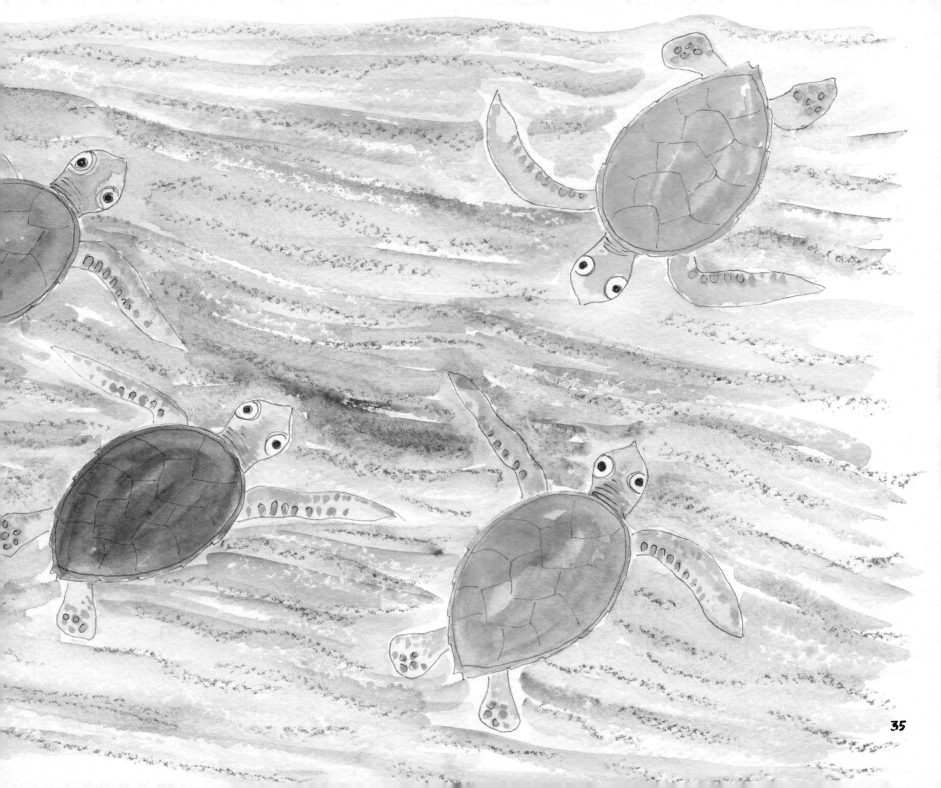

They swam on, all talking at once, telling tales of
their adventures so far. They didn't even notice as
the land grew smaller, disappearing in the distance.
They were travelling on the ocean currents far out
to sea - and they were happy hatchlings, ready to
explore their exciting new world ...